TWAIN
Illustrated

Adapted Classics for Middle School
An imprint of ArtWrite Productions
1555 Gardena Ave NE
Minneapolis, MN 55432-5848

Book Design by ArtWrite Productions
Edited by John Leitner
Cover Design by Kristina Brown

ISBN 978-1-939846-25-9

adaptedclassics.com

kristinadesignz.com

artwriteproductions.com

TWAIN Illustrated

THREE STORIES BY MARK TWAIN

ADAPTED BY:
JEROME TILLER
ILLUSTRATED BY:
MARC JOHNSON-PENCOOK

The *Adapted Classics* Collection

Contemporary-classic illustrations in *Adapted Classics* books add expression to visually-rich stories by world-famous authors. Lightly modified and illustrated to suit and attract modern young readers, stories in the *Adapted Classics* collection are respectful renditions of timeless stories from the world of classic literature.

View the entire collection at: www.adaptedclassics.com

PREFACE

You are about to read adapted versions of three stories by Mark Twain, one of the world's all-time greatest authors. Some changes (paragraph breaks, rearrangements, minor additions and omissions, etc.) were made to accommodate the illustration of characters and critical scenes in the stories. Some changes (word choice, word order, etc.) were made to expand its accessibility and appeal, keeping modern youth in mind. No change was made with the notion it would improve the text or the story.

Among other places, the original version of each story can be found at: http://www.gutenberg.org/

CONTENTS

EMERSON, HOLMES, & LONGFELLOW

(AKA – TWAIN'S DECEMBER 17, 1877 SPEECH AT THE HOTEL BRUNSWICK, BOSTON)

Samuel Clemens is my name, but I sought my fame in literary circles as Mark Twain, the pen-name I adopted. It wasn't long after Mark Twain had stirred up a literary puddle in Nevada that I became conceited. I decided to tramp through the southern mines of California to see how thickly the vapor of my fame had penetrated there, thoroughly resolved to try out the virtue of my pen-name.

I very soon had an opportunity. I knocked at a miner's lonely log cabin in the foothills of the Sierras just at nightfall. It was snowing at the time. A jaded, melancholy man of fifty, barefooted, opened the door to me. When he heard my pen-name he looked more dejected than before. He let me in—pretty reluctantly, I thought—and after the customary bacon and beans, black coffee and hot cider, I took a pipe.

This sorrowful man had not said three words up to this time. Now he spoke up and said in the voice of one who is secretly suffering, "You're the fourth—I'm going to move."

"The fourth what?" said I.

"The fourth littery man that has been here in twenty-four hours—I'm going to move."

"You don't tell me!" said I. "Who were the others?"

"Mr. Henry Longfellow, Mr. Ralph Waldo Emerson, and Mr. Oliver Wendell Holmes—consound the lot!"

You can easily believe I was interested. I earnestly begged to hear more, and after three hot ciders, the melancholy miner finally began.

"They came here just at dark yesterday evening, and I let them in of course. Said they were going to the Yosemite. They were a rough lot, but that's nothing; everybody looks rough that travels afoot. Mr. Emerson was a seedy little bit of a chap, red-headed. Mr. Holmes was as fat as a balloon; he weighed as much as three hundred and had double chins all the way down to his stomach. Mr. Longfellow was built like a prize-fighter. His head was cropped and bristly, like as if he had a wig made of hair-brushes. His nose lay straight down his face, like a finger with the end joint tilted up."

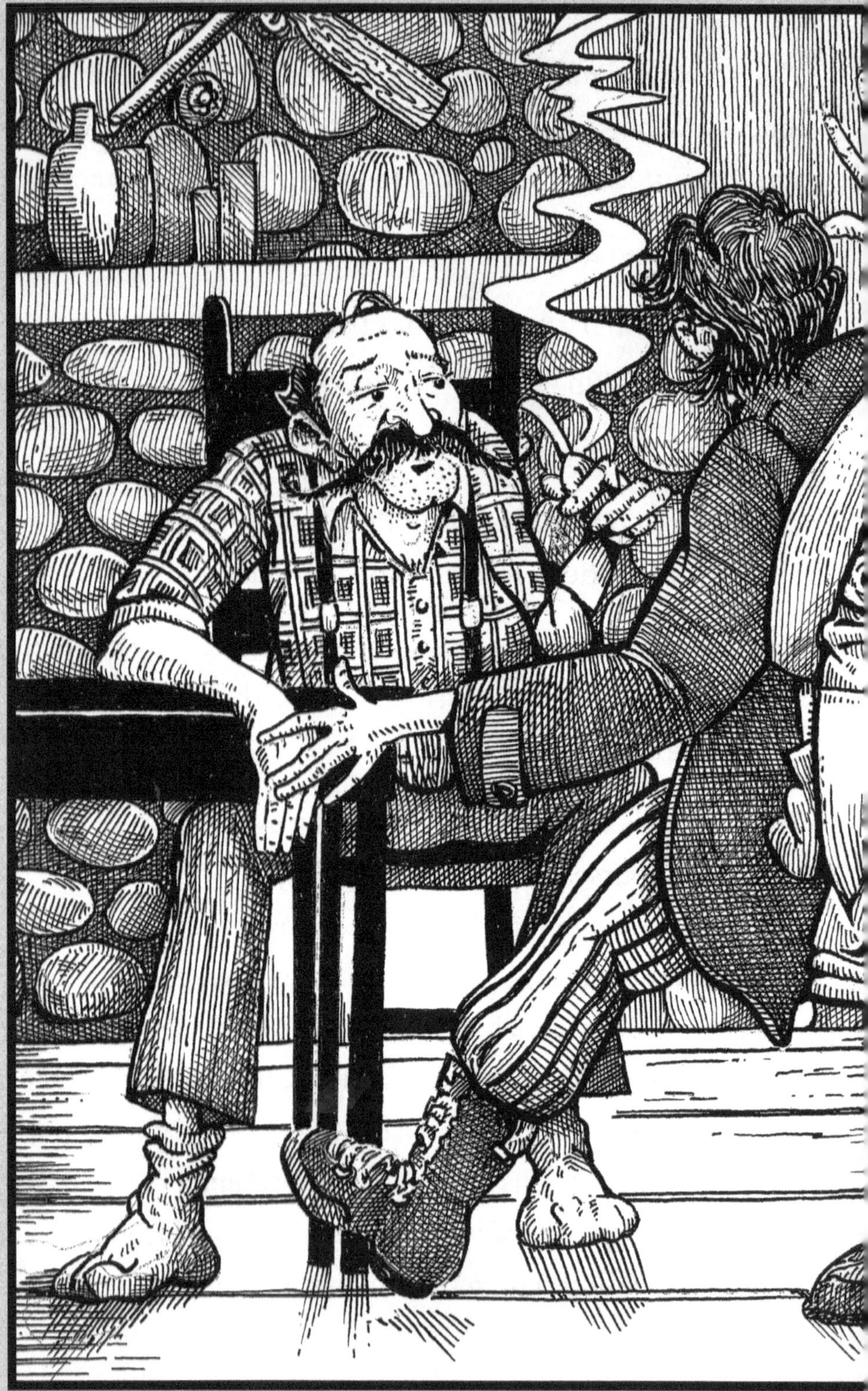

“They had been drinking, I could see that. And what queer talk they used! Mr. Holmes inspected this cabin, then he took me by the buttonhole, and says he:

‘While on mine ear it rings,
Through the deep caves of thought
I hear a voice that sings,
Build thee more stately mansions,
O my soul!’”

"Says I, 'I can't afford it, Mr. Holmes, and moreover I don't want to.' Blamed me if I liked what he had said neither, coming from a stranger that way.”

“However, I started to get out my bacon and beans, when Mr. Emerson came and looked on awhile, and then he takes me aside by the buttonhole and says:

‘Give me agates for my meat;
Give me beetles to eat;
From air and ocean bring me foods,
From all zones and altitudes.
From all natures, sharp and slimy,
Bird and reptile, wild and tame.
Ape and sea-lion, be my game.’”

“Mr. Emerson,’ says I, ‘if you'll excuse me, this ain't no hotel.’”

"You see it sort of riled me—I warn't used to the ways of littery swells. But I went on a-sweating over my work, and next comes Mr. Longfellow, who buttonholes and interrupts me with some dang song of Hiawatha. Says he:

'Honor be to Mudjekeewis!
Ruler of the winds of heaven.
You shall hear how Pau-Puk-Keewis,
He, the handsome Storm-Fool,
Vexed the village with disturbance.'"

"But I broke in and says, 'I beg your pardon, Mr. Longfellow, if you'll be so kind as to hold your yawp for about five minutes and let me get this grub ready, you'll do me proud.'"

"Well, sir, after they'd filled up I set out the jug of cider. Mr. Holmes looks at it, and then he fires up all of a sudden and yells:

'Flash out a stream of blood-red wine!
For I would drink to other days.'"

"By George, I was getting kind of worked up. I don't deny it, I was getting kind of worked up. I turns to Mr. Holmes, and says I, 'Looky here my fat friend, I'm a-running this shanty, and if the court knows herself, you'll take cider or you'll go dry.'"

"Them's the very words I said to him. Now I don't want to sass such famous littery people, but you see they kind of forced me. There ain't nothing unreasonable 'bout me; I don't mind a passel of guests treadin' on my tail three or four times. But when it comes to standing on it, that's different."

"Anyway', says I, 'and if the court knows herself, you'll take cider or you'll go dry.'"

"Well, between drinks they'd swell around the cabin and strike attitudes and spout. And pretty soon they got out a greasy old deck of cards and went to playing showdown poker at ten cents an ante—on trust. I began to notice some pretty suspicious things. Mr. Emerson dealt, but all the hands he put down only within reach of himself. He looked at his hand, shook his head, and says:

'I am the doubter and the doubt.'"

"Next he calmly bunched the hands he had just dealt and went to shuffling for a new layout. Says he:

'They reckon ill who leave me out;
They know now well the subtle ways I keep.
I pass and deal again!'"

"Hang'd if he didn't go ahead and do it, too! Oh, he was a cool one! Well, in a minute things were running pretty tight, but all of a sudden I see by Mr. Emerson's eye he judged he had 'em. He had already corralled two pots on trust, and each of the others got one. So now he kind of lifts a little in his chair and says:

'I tire of globes and aces!
Too long the game is played!' "

"And down he laid a full boat, kings over threes. Mr. Longfellow smiles as sweet as pie and says:

'Thanks, thanks to thee, my worthy friend,
For the lesson thou has taught.' "

"Then blamed if he didn't throw down a full boat of his own, kings over fours! "

"Emerson claps his hand on his bowie knife, Longfellow claps his on his revolver, and I went under a bunk. There was going to be trouble. But that monstrous Holmes rose up, wobbling his double chins, and says he, 'Order, gentlemen. The first man that draws, I'll lay down on him and smother him!'"

"All quiet on the western front, you bet! But all that and otherwise, they had been so pretty well along into 'how-come-you-dirty rat' by then that they begun to blow."

"Emerson says, 'The knobbiest thing I ever wrote was *Barbara Frietchie*.'"

"Says Longfellow, 'It don't out-knob my *Biglow Papers*'"

"Says Holmes, 'My *Thanatopsis* lays over 'em both.'"

"They mighty near ended in a fight. Then they wished they had some more company—and Mr. Emerson pointed to me and says:

'Is yonder squalid peasant all
That this proud nursery could breed?'"

"He was a-whetting his bowie knife on his boot—so I let the insult pass. Well, sir, next they took it into their heads that they would like some music. So they made me stand up and sing *When Johnny Comes Marching Home* till I dropped—at thirteen minutes past four this morning."

"That's what I've been through, my friend. When I woke at seven, they were leaving, thank goodness, and Mr. Longfellow had my only pair of boots on his feet and his own boots under his arm."

XXX

"Says I, 'Hold on there, Evangeline, what are you going to do with my boots?'"

"He says, 'Going to make tracks with 'em because:

> 'Lives of great men all remind us
> We can make our lives sublime;
> And, departing, leave behind us
> Footprints on the sands of time.'''

"As I said, Mr. Twain, you are the fourth in twenty-four hours—and I'm going to move; I ain't suited to a littery atmosphere."

I said to the miner, "Why, my dear sir, these were not the gracious singers to whom we and the world pay loving reverence and homage. These men were impostors."

The miner investigated me with a calm eye for a while; then said he, "Ah! impostors, were they? Are you?"

I did not pursue the subject, and since then I have not traveled on my pen-name enough to hurt.

the end

EMERSON, HOLMES, & LONGFELLOW

(AKA TWAIN'S DECEMBER 17, 1877 SPEECH AT HOTEL BRUNSWICK, BOSTON, MA)

In 1877 Mark Twain attended a banquet to celebrate the 70th birthday of John Greenleaf Whittier, a famous American poet. Three other famous American poets also sat with Whittier at the head table—Ralph Waldo Emerson, Oliver Wendall Holmes, and Henry Wadsworth Longfellow. Twain was there to give a speech that would entertain them and a roomful of guests. Although he did deliver a speech, he spent the next 28 years refusing to remember that he had. According to Twain, nobody laughed or smiled, not once, all the way through to the end of the speech. Rather, the entire audience seemed turned to stone with horror. By the time Twain sat down after completing the speech, he said his heart had long ceased to beat. He said he was never as miserable again as he was then. He never could account for their reaction, or lack thereof. After he reviewed the speech almost three decades later, he found no fault with it.

The humor his audience apparently missed lies mostly in two areas: mistaken identity and flawed interpretation. Both types are similar. Roughly, when a listener or reader is knowledgeable and able to make connections with material as presented, it's amusing to follow a character in a story who is unable to do the same.

Much of the mistaken-identity humor in this piece would be lost on modern readers. In 1877, many Americans got their entertainment listening to family members recite poems. Many people knew a number of poems by heart and could identify many more because they had read or heard them in school. They would know that some of the famous poems Twain used in the piece were written by poets other than the impostors he put into the cabin with the miner.

As for the flawed-interpretation humor, the miner doesn't know any poetry, so even modern readers find it humorous when he interprets his visitor's verse as if they were spouting common lingo. Besides that, he assertively mocks and calls out the arrogant characters he was hosting, and there is perpetual appeal in that kind of discourse. Finally, there's the self-deprecation in the last line—Samuel Clemens traveling as Mark Twain was an impostor of sorts himself!

THE FACTS CONCERNING THE RECENT CARNIVAL OF CRIME IN CONNECTICUT

This morning as I put a match to my cigar, Aunt Mary came to mind. I was hungry to see her again. Outside of my own household, she was the person I loved and honored most in all the world. She had been my boyhood's idol, and time had not dislodged her from her pedestal. Rather, it had only justified her right to be there and placed her dethronement permanently among the impossibilities.

Her influence over me was so strong that long after everybody else's "do-stop-smoking" had ceased to affect me in the slightest degree, Aunt Mary still could stir my dormant conscience into faint signs of life whenever she mentioned my smoking habit.

But all things have their limit in this world. A happy day came at last when even Aunt Mary's words about smoking could no longer move me. That day arrived during her visit one winter ago, and I was more than glad it did; for when the sun had set on that happy day, the one thing that could mar my enjoyment of my aunt's company was gone. The remainder of her stay with us that winter was in every way a delight. Of course, even after that blessed day she pleaded with me to quit my hurtful habit just as earnestly as she ever had, but to no purpose whatever. The moment she opened the subject, I at once became calmly, peacefully, contentedly indifferent—absolutely unbudgingly indifferent. Consequently, I could not have enjoyed my pet vice more if my gentle tormentor had been a smoker herself, and an advocate of the practice.

As I smoked my cigar while recalling these things, the morning mail came in. Quite coincidentally, the first envelope I noticed was addressed in Aunt Mary's handwriting. The sight of it sent a thrill of pleasure through and through me. I easily guessed what I should find in her letter. I opened it. Good—just as I expected; she was coming! Coming this very day, too, and by the morning train; I might expect her any moment.

"Ah, what a wonderful life," I said to myself as I launched a smoke ring into the air and watched it sail away. "I am so thoroughly happy and content now, that if my most pitiless enemy could appear before me at this moment, I would freely right any wrong I may have done him."

Straightaway the door opened, and a shriveled, shabby, itty-bitty man entered. He was not more than two feet high. He seemed to be about forty years old. Every feature and every inch of him was a trifle out of shape; and so while you could not put a finger upon any particular part and say, 'this is a conspicuous deformity', any spectator would perceive that this little person was a deformity as a whole—a vague, general, evenly blended, nicely adjusted deformity.

There was a fox-like cunning in the face and the sharp little eyes, and also alertness and malice. And yet, this vile bit of human rubbish seemed to bear a sort of remote and ill-defined resemblance to me! It was dully perceptible in the form and face, and even the clothes, gestures, manner, and attitudes of the creature. He was a far-fetched, dim suggestion of a burlesque upon me—a caricature of me in little. Two things about him struck me most unpleasantly: he was covered all over with a fuzzy, greenish mold, such as one sometimes sees upon mildewed bread, and he was sprouting fungi! The sight of him was nauseating.

He stepped along with a chipper air, and flung himself into a doll's chair in a very free-and-easy way, without waiting to be asked. He tossed his hat into the waste-basket. He picked up my old chalk pipe from the floor, gave the stem a wipe or two on his knee, filled the bowl from the tobacco-box at his side, and said to me in a tone of pert command: "Gimme a match!"

I blushed to the roots of my hair, partly with anger, but mainly because it seemed to me that his whole performance was an exaggeration of conduct I had sometimes been guilty of myself. I wanted to thrash him for that mockery, but a strange sense of being under his control forced me to obey his order.

He applied the match to my pipe, took a thoughtful whiff or two, and remarked, in an irritatingly familiar way: "Seems to me it's devilish odd weather for this time of year."

I flushed again in anger and humiliation, for the language he used was just like some that I have uttered in my day. Moreover, he spoke in a tone of voice and with a drawl that seemed to deliberately distort my style. Now there is nothing that so disturbs me as a mocking imitation of my slow, drawling speech. I spoke up sharply and said:

"Look here, you miserable ash-cat! You will have to pay a little more attention to your manners or I will throw you out of the window!"

The despicable creature smiled a smile of malicious content and security. Puffing a whiff of smoke toward me with contempt, he said, in a still more elaborate drawl: "Come—go gently now. And don't put on too many airs with your betters."

This cool snub grated me all over. But it also seemed to conquer me for a moment. The measly one looked me over for awhile with his weasel eyes and then said in a sneering way:

"You turned a poor man away from your door this morning, didn't ya?"

I replied harshly:"Perhaps I did and perhaps I didn't. How do you know?"

"Well, I know. It doesn't matter how I know."

"Very well. Suppose I did turn a hobo away from the door—what of it?"

"Oh, nothing in particular. Only you lied to him."

"I didn't! That is, I—"

"Yes. Yes, you did. You lied to him."

I felt a guilty pang. In truth, I had felt guilty forty times before that poor man had walked a block from my door. Still, I made a show of feeling slandered, saying: "This is a baseless insult. I said to the man—"

"There—hold on. You were about to lie again. I know what you said to him. You said the cook was gone and there was nothing left from breakfast. Two lies. You knew the cook was behind the door and you knew there were plenty of provisions behind her."

This astonishing accuracy silenced me, and it filled me with wondering speculations, too. How could he have gotten his information? Of course he could have spoken with the man, but by what sort of magic could he have found out about the cook concealed behind the door?

Now the mini-man spoke again: "It was rather pitiful, rather small, of you to refuse to read that poor young woman's story the other day and give her your opinion on its literary value. And she had come so far and with so much hope."

I felt like a dog! And I had felt so every time the thing had recurred to my mind, I may as well confess. I flushed hotly and said: "Look here, have you nothing better to do than prowl around prying into other people's business? Did that girl tell you that?"

"Never mind whether she did or not. The main thing is that you did a mean thing. And you felt ashamed of it afterward. Aha! You feel ashamed of it now!"

He said this with a sort of devilish glee. With fiery earnestness I responded:

"I told that girl, in the kindest, gentlest way, that I could not deliver judgment upon anyone's written work because an individual's verdict was worthless. I might underrate a work of high merit and lose it to the world, or I might overrate a trashy production and open the way for it to be inflicted upon the world. I told her that the great, general public was the only jury competent to sit in judgment upon a literary effort, and therefore it would be best to lay her work before the public at the outset, since in the end it must stand or fall by their decision anyway."

"Yes, you said all that. So you did, you juggling, small-souled shuffler! And yet when the happy hopefulness faded out of that poor girl's face, when you saw her slowly sneak beneath her shawl the scroll she had so patiently and honestly scribbled at—so ashamed of her darling now, so proud of it before—when you saw the gladness go out of her eyes and the tears well up there, when she, who had come so far, crept away so humbly—"

"Oh, peace! Peace! Peace! Blister your merciless tongue! Haven't all these thoughts tortured me enough without your fetching them back again!"

Remorse! Remorse! Remorse! It seemed to me that remorse would eat the very heart out of me! And yet that small fiend only sat there leering at me with joy and contempt, chuckling peacefully.

Presently he began to speak again. Every sentence was an accusation and every accusation a truth. Every clause was loaded with sarcasm and derision, every slow-dropping word burned like acid. The miniature man reminded me

of times when I had flown at my children in anger and punished them for bad deeds that, with just a little inquiry, I would have known they had not committed. He reminded me of how I had disloyally allowed old friends to be slandered in my hearing without uttering a word in their defense. He reminded me of many dishonest things I had done and many others that I had gotten children and other irresponsible persons to do for me, and of others that I had planned, thought upon, and longed to do, and been kept from doing by fear of consequences only. With exquisite cruelty he recalled to my mind, item by item, wrongs, unkindnesses, and humiliations I had inflicted upon friends since dead, "who died thinking of those injuries, maybe, and grieving over them," he said, adding poison to the stab.

"For instance," said he, "take the case of your younger brother. Many a long year ago when you two were boys together, he lovingly trusted you with a faithfulness that your many and varied treacheries were not able to shake. He followed you about like a dog, content to suffer wrong and abuse if he might only be with you and patient under these injuries so long as it was your hand that inflicted them. Remember when you pledged your honor that, if he would let you blindfold him, no harm should come to him. And then, giggling and choking over the rare fun of the joke, you led him to a brook thinly glazed with ice and pushed him in. And oh, how you did laugh! Man, if you live a thousand years you will never forget the gentle, reproachful look he gave you as he struggled shivering out of that brook. Oh! You see it now! You see it now!"

"Beast, I have seen it a million times over and shall see it a million more! And may you rot away piecemeal and suffer till doomsday what I suffer now for bringing it back to me again!"

The mini-man chuckled contentedly and went on with his accusing history of my life. I dropped into a moody, vengeful state, and suffered in silence under the merciless lash, until a remark that gave me a sudden awakening!

"Two months ago, on a Tuesday, you woke up in the middle of the night and fell to thinking, with shame, about a peculiarly mean and pitiful act of yours toward a man you abandoned in the—"

"Stop a moment, devil! Stop! Up until now you've been telling me about my actions. Do you mean to tell me now that even my very thoughts are not hidden from you?"

"It seems to look like that. Didn't you think the thoughts I have just mentioned?"

"If I didn't may I never breathe again! Look here, friend—look me in the eye. Who are you?"

"Well, who do you think?"

"I think you are Satan himself. You are the devil."

"No."

"No? Then who can you be?"

"Would you really like to know?"

"Indeed I would."

"Well, I am your Conscience!"

In an instant I was in a blaze of joy and exultation. I sprang at the creature, roaring:

"Curse you, I have wished a hundred million times that you were tangible and that I could get my hands on your throat just once! Oh, but now I will wreak a deadly vengeance on—"

Folly! Lightning does not move more quickly than my Conscience did! He darted aloft so suddenly that, in the moment my fingers clutched the empty air, he was already perched on the top of the high bookcase thumbing his nose at me in a token of derision.

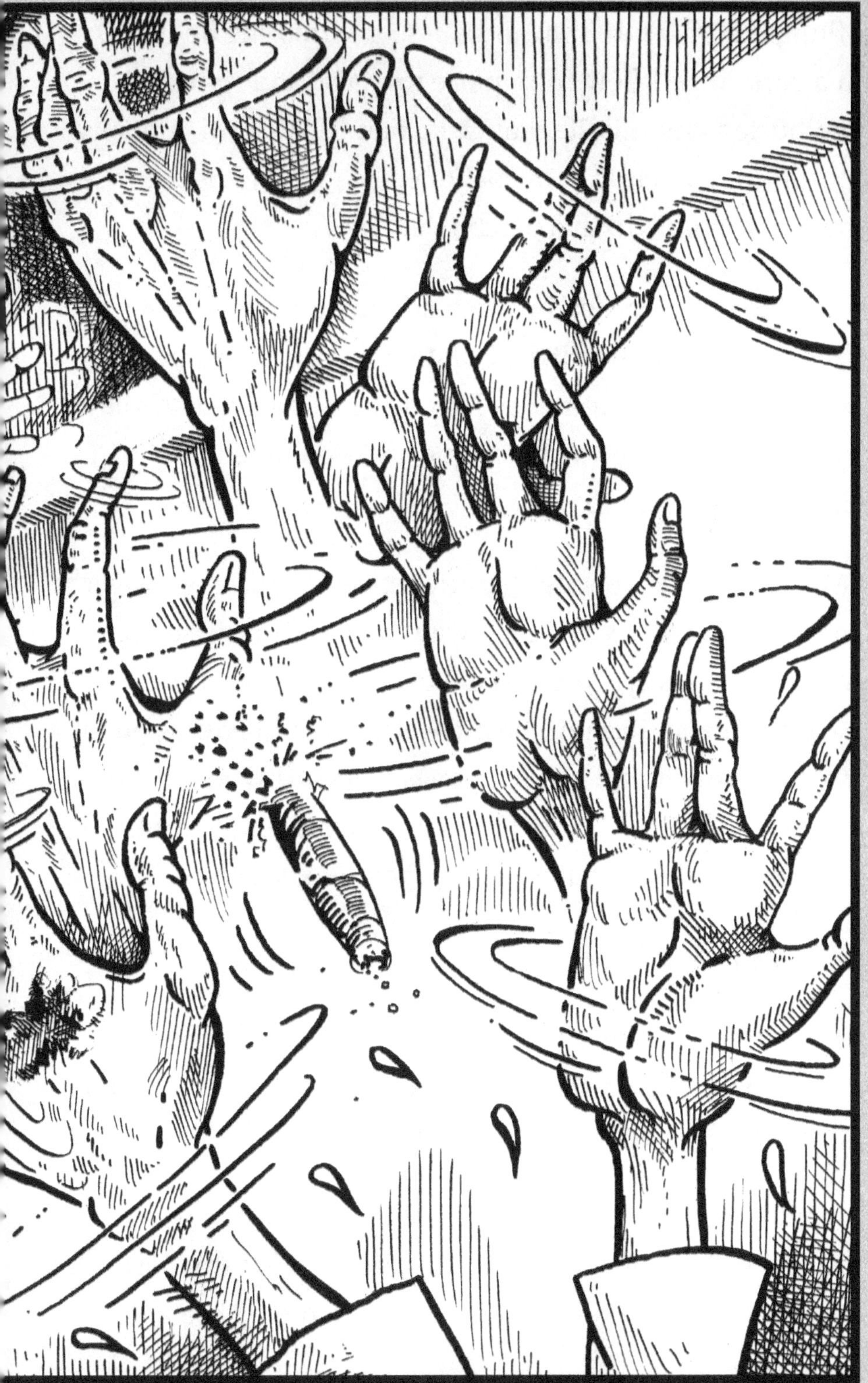

I flung the poker at him, and missed. I fired the bootjack. In a blind rage I flew from place to place, and snatched and hurled any missile that came handy. A storm of books, inkstands, and chunks of coal filled the air and beat about the measly munchkin's perch relentlessly.

But all to no purpose; the nimble figure dodged every shot. And not only that, he burst into a cackle of sarcastic and triumphant laughter as I sat down exhausted. While I puffed and gasped with fatigue and excitement, my Conscience talked to me.

"My good slave, you are characteristically witless—always consistent, always yourself, always a fool. Otherwise you would have known you needed to attempt this murder with a sad heart and a heavy conscience. You could have brought me down low if you had felt pangs of guilt. I would have drooped under the burden instantly. I would have weighed a ton and could not have budged from the floor."

"You mean to tell me that—"

"You are so anxious to destroy me that your conscience is as light as a feather. Hence, I am away up here out of your reach, in the air and free as a bird.

I would have given anything right then to be heavy-hearted so I could get this creature down from up there and do away with him. But I could no more be heavy-hearted over a desire to thrash him than I could have been sorrowful over doing it. As it was, I could only look longingly up at my master and rave at the ill luck that denied me a heavy conscience the one and only time I had ever wanted such a thing in my life.

By and by I got to musing over the hour's strange adventure, and of course my human curiosity began to work. I set to framing in my mind some questions for this fiend to answer. Just then one of my girls entered, leaving the door open behind her.

"My! What has been going on here? The bookcase is all one riddle of—"

I sprang up in panic and shouted:"Out of here! Hurry! Shut the door! Quick, or my Conscience will get away!"

The door slammed, and I locked it. I glanced up and was grateful, to the bottom of my heart, to see that my owner was still my prisoner.

"Hang you, I might have lost you! Children are the most carefree creatures. But look here, friend, the girl did not seem to notice you at all. How is that?"

"For a very good reason. I am invisible to all but you."

I made a mental note of that piece of information with a good deal of satisfaction: I could destroy this villain now, if I got a chance and no one would know it. But this happy thought made me so lighthearted that my Conscience could hardly keep himself seated atop the bookcase—he was like to float aloft toward the ceiling like a toy balloon.

"Come, my Conscience, let us be friendly. Let us fly a flag of truce for a while. I am suffering to ask you some questions."

"Very well. Begin."

"Well, then, in the first place, why were you never visible to me before?"

"Because you never asked to see me before. That is, you never asked in the right spirit and proper form before. You were in just the right spirit this time when you sat back in your chair, blew smoke rings in the air, and called out for your most pitiless enemy. Although you didn't suspect it, that person was me by a very large majority, and so I appeared."

"Well, did my remark turn you into flesh and blood?"

"No. It only made me visible to you. I am without substance, the same as other spirits."

This remark prodded me with a sharp misgiving. If he was bodiless, how was I going to kill him? But I dissembled, and said persuasively:

"Conscience, it isn't sociable of you to keep at such a distance. Come down off that bookcase and take another smoke."

This was answered with a look that was full of derision: "Come where you can get at me and kill me? The invitation is declined, with thanks."

"All right," said I to myself; "so it seems a spirit can be killed, after all. Good! There will be one spirit lacking in this world, presently, or I lose my guess." Then I said aloud: "Friend—"

"There, wait a bit. I am not your friend. I am your enemy. I am not your equal, I am your master. Call me 'my lord,' if you please. You are being too familiar."

"I don't like such overblown titles. I am willing to call you sir. That is as far as—"

"We will have no argument about this. Just obey, that is all. Go on with your chatter."

"Very well, my lord—since nothing but 'my lord' will suit you—I was going to ask you how long you will be visible to me?"

"Always!"

"This is simply an outrage. That is what I think of it! You have dogged and dogged and dogged me all the days of my life, invisible. That was misery enough! But now to have such a foul-looking thing as you tagging after me like another shadow all the rest of my days? That is an intolerable prospect!"

"My lad, there was never so pleased a conscience in this world as I was when you made me visible. It gives me an inconceivable advantage. Now I can look you straight in the eye and call you names, and leer at you, jeer at you, and sneer at you. And you know what eloquence there is in visible gesture and expression, especially when the effect is heightened by audible speech. Henceforth I will always address you in your own s-n-i-v-e-l-i-n-g d-r-a-w-l, baby!"

I let fly with the coal-hod. No result. My lord said:

"Come, come! Remember the flag of truce!"

"Ah, I forgot that. I will try to be civil, and you try it, too, for a novelty. The idea of a civil conscience! It is a good joke; an excellent joke. All the consciences I have ever heard of were nagging, badgering, fault-finding, detestable savages! Yes; and always in a sweat about some poor little insignificant trifle or other. May destruction catch the lot of them, I say! I would trade mine for the smallpox and seven kinds of consumption and be glad of the chance. Now tell me, why is it that a conscience can't haul a man over the coals once, for an offense, and then let him alone? Why is it that a conscience wants to keep on pegging at him, day and night and night and day, week in and week out, forever and ever, about the same old thing? There is no sense in

that. I think a conscience that will act like that is meaner than the very dirt itself."

"Well, *we* like it; that suffices."

"Do you do it with the honest intent to improve a person?"

That question produced a sarcastic smile, and this reply: "No, sir. Excuse me. We do it simply because it is 'business'. It is our trade. The purpose of it is to improve the person, but we are merely disinterested agents. We are appointed by authority and haven't anything to say in the matter. We obey orders and leave the consequences where they belong. But I am willing to admit this much: we do crowd the orders a trifle when we get a chance, which is most of the time. We enjoy it. We are instructed to remind a man a few times of an error, and I don't mind acknowledging that we try to give pretty good measure. And when we get hold of a man of a peculiarly sensitive nature, oh, but we do haze him! I have had consciences come all the way from China and Russia to see a person of that kind put through his paces, on a special occasion."

"Well, aren't you a precious crew, not to put it too strongly. In your anxiety to get all the juice you can out of a sin, you make a man repent of it in three or four different ways."

"That does please us a bit, I admit"

"And that explains why you have always been a trifle inconsistent! You found fault with me for lying to that hobo, and I suffered over it. But it was only yesterday that I told a charity worker the square truth. I told him that it was regarded as bad citizenship to encourage welfare, so I would give him nothing. What did you do then? Why, you made me say to myself, 'Ah, it would have been so much kinder and more blameless to ease him off with a little white lie about being out of cash and send him away feeling that, if he could not get any money out of me, then at least my compassion toward his cause was something to be grateful for!'"

"And that bothered you?"

"I suffered all day about it. But three days before that, I gave money freely to a charity worker, supposing it a virtuous act. Straight off you said to me, 'Oh, false citizen, to have supported welfare!' And I suffered, as usual. Then I gave a poor man a job for pay and you objected to that—after the contract was made, of course; you never speak up beforehand. Next, I refused a poor man work. You objected to that. Next, I proposed to kill a persistent beggar, and you kept me awake all night, oozing remorse at every pore. Then, positively sure that I was going to be right, I sent the next beggar away with my benediction; I wish you may live as long as I do if you didn't make me smart all night again because I didn't thrash him. Is there any way of satisfying that malignant invention which is called a conscience?"

"Ha, ha! This is luxury! Go on!"

"But come now, answer me. Is there any way?"

"Well, none that I propose to tell you, my son. I don't care what act you may turn your hand to, I can straightway whisper a word in your ear and make you think you have committed a dreadful meanness. It is my business—and my joy—to make you repent of everything you do. If I have fooled away any opportunities, it was not intentional!"

"Don't worry; you haven't missed a trick that I know of. I never did a thing in all my life, even virtuous things, that I didn't repent of in twenty-four hours. In church last Sunday I listened to a charity sermon. My first impulse was to give three hundred and fifty dollars; I repented of that and reduced it a hundred; repented of that and reduced it another hundred; repented of that and reduced it another hundred; repented of that and reduced the remaining fifty to twenty-five; repented of that and came down to fifteen; repented of that and dropped it to two dollars and a half. When the plate came around at last, I repented once more and contributed ten cents. Well, when I got home, I wished to goodness I had that ten cents back! You never did let me get through a charity sermon without having something to sweat about."

"Oh, and I never shall, I never shall. You can always depend on me."

"I think so. Many and many is the restless night I've wanted to take you by the neck. If I could only get hold of you now!"

"Yes, no doubt. But I am not a dumb ox. I am only the yoke of a dumb ox. But go on, go on. You entertain me more than I like to confess."

"I am glad of that. (You will not mind my lying a little to keep in practice.) Look here; not to be too personal, I think you are about the shabbiest and most contemptible little shriveled-up reptile that can be imagined. I am grateful enough that you are invisible to other people, for I should die with shame to be seen with such a mildewed monkey of a conscience as you are. Now if you were five or six feet high, and—"

"Oh, come! Who is to blame?"

"I don't know."

"Why, you are—nobody else."

"Confound you, I wasn't consulted about your height or personal appearance."

"I don't care. You had a good deal to do with it, nevertheless. When you were eight or nine years old, I was seven feet high, and as pretty as a picture."

"I wish you had died young! So you have grown the wrong way, have you?"

"Some of us grow one way and some the other. It depends on how successful we are. You had a large conscience once; there are reasons you have a small conscience now. However, both of us are to blame for it, you and I. You see, you used to be conscientious about a great many things. Excessively so, I may say. That was a great many years ago; you probably do not remember it now. Well, I took a great interest in my work and so enjoyed the anguish you suffered over certain pet sins that I kept pelting you with more anguish until I rather overdid the matter. You began to rebel, which caused me to shrink a little, then I shrunk still more as you persisted to rebel."

Then it's all on you! You shrunk because you overdid the matter! But you are so disgustingly ugly as well! Who is to blame for that?

I shriveled when I shrunk—that's part of it. As for the callouses, it was your precious pet sins that caused them to grow. Yes, I pelted anguish at you unmercifully for your pet sins trying to get you to reform—or at least improve. But you rebelled so strongly, so often, that I weakened. Not only did I shrivel, I got moldy, pushed up mushrooms, and grew deformed in other ways. And the more I weakened and deteriorated, the more stubbornly you fastened onto your pet sins, until at last the places on my person that mark your pet vices became as callous as armadillo-skin. Take smoking for instance. I played that card too long, you rebelled, and I surrendered. Of late when people plead with you to quit smoking, you instinctively close your mind and ignore their pleas. That spurs your smoking-vice callous to grow, which smothers me, and I go sound asleep. Sound asleep? Sound is no name for it. I couldn't hear it thunder at such a time. You have developed some few other vices—perhaps eighty, or maybe ninety—that affect me in much the same way."

"This is flattering! You must be asleep a good part of your time."

"Yes, of late years. I should be asleep all the time but for the help I get."

"Who helps you to stay awake?"

"Other consciences. If a conscience I know is assigned to a person who begins pleading with you about a vice you are callous to, I get my colleague to give the pleading person a pang of guilt concerning a vice that he or she has. That usually stops the meddling and restores my wakefulness. On my own, without the help of other consciences, my useful advocacy with you is about trimmed down to the fields of giving: generosity, kindness, helpfulness—that line of goods. But don't you worry—I will harry you about your social obligations as long as I can! You just put your trust in me."

"I think I can. But if you had only been good enough to mention these facts some thirty years ago, I would have turned my particular attention to sin of all kinds. I think that by this time I would not only have had you permanently asleep on the entire list of human vices, but shrunk to the size of a pill at that. That is about the style of conscience I am pining for. And if I had shrunk you down to a pill and could get my hands on you, then what do you think? Would I put you in a glass case for a keepsake? No, sir. I would feed you to a snake in the grass! That is where you ought to be—you and all your tribe. You are not fit to be in society, in my opinion. Now another question. Do you know a good many consciences in this section?"

"Plenty of them."

"I would give anything to see some of them! Could you bring them here? And would they be visible to me?"

"Certainly not."

"I suppose I ought to have known that without asking. But no matter, you can describe them. Tell me about my neighbor Thompson's conscience, please."

"Very well. I know him intimately—have known him many years. I knew him when he was eleven feet high and a faultless figure. But he is very pasty and tough and misshapen now, and hardly ever interests himself about anything. As to his present size—well, he sleeps in a cigar-box."

"Likely enough. There are few smaller, meaner men in this region than Hugh Thompson. Do you know Robinson's conscience?"

"Yes. He is a shade under four and a half feet high. He used to be a blond. He's a brunette now, but still shapely and handsome."

"Well, Robinson is a good fellow. Do you know Tom Smith's conscience?"

"I have known him from childhood. He was thirteen inches high and rather sluggish when he was two years old—as nearly all of us are at that age. He is thirty-seven feet high now, firmly grounded, and the stateliest figure in America. Never sleeps. He is the most active and energetic member of the New England Conscience Club. Night and day you can find him pegging away at Smith, panting with his labor, sleeves rolled up, face alive with enjoyment. He can make poor Smith imagine the least little thing he does is a disgusting sin, then he sets to work and almost tortures the soul out of him about it. Smith's conscience has attained his height and fame because he is so effective at making Smith a righteous, yet humble man. He has got his victim whipped into splendid shape, but still he persists, growing larger and larger. His legs are racked with growing-pains, but he has a good time, nevertheless."

"Smith is the noblest man in all this section, and the purest. Yet he is always breaking his heart because he cannot be good enough! Only a conscience could find pleasure in heaping agony upon a man like that. Do you know my Aunt Mary's conscience?"

"I have seen her at a distance, but I'm not acquainted with her. She lives altogether in the open air because no door is large enough to admit her."

"I can believe that. Let me see. Do you know the conscience of that adapter Jerome Tiller who once stole some sketches of mine for a 'series' of his and left me with nothing in royalties?"

"Yes. That conscience is totally infamous. He was exhibited a month ago. Tickets and fares were high, but I traveled for nothing by pretending to be the conscience of a politician, then got in for half-price by representing myself to be the conscience of a clergyman. However, the adapter's conscience, which was to have been the main feature of the entertainment, was a failure as an exhibition. He was there, but what of it? Management had provided a microscope with a magnifying power of only thirty thousand diameters, so nobody got to see him, after all. There was great and general dissatisfaction, of course, but—"

Just here there was an eager footstep on the stair. I opened the door and my Aunt Mary burst into the room. It was a joyful meeting and a cheery bombardment of questions and answers concerning family matters ensued.

By and by my aunt said: "I am going to abuse you a little now. You promised me, the day I saw you last, that you would look after the needs of the poor family around the corner as faithfully as I had done it myself. Well, I found out by accident that you failed of your promise. Is that right?"

In simple truth, I never had thought of that family a second time! And now such a splintering pang of guilt shot through me! I glanced up at my Conscience high upon the bookcase. Plainly, my heavy heart was weighing on him. His body was drooping forward; he seemed about to fall. My aunt continued:

"And think how you have neglected the poor girl I sponsor at the almshouse, you dear, hard-hearted promise-breaker!"

I blushed scarlet, and my tongue was tied. As the sense of my guilty negligence waxed sharper and stronger, my Conscience began to sway heavily back and forth.

And then my aunt, after a little pause, said in a grieved tone, "Since you never once went to see her, maybe it will not bother you now to know that poor child died, months ago, utterly friendless and forsaken!"

My Conscience could no longer bear up under the weight of my suffering guilt. He tumbled headlong from his high perch and struck the floor with a dull, leaden thump. He lay there writhing with pain and quaking with apprehension, but straining every muscle in frantic efforts to get up.

In a fever of expectancy I sprang to the door, locked it, placed my back against it, and bent a watchful gaze upon my struggling master. Already my fingers were itching to begin their murderous work.

"Oh, what can be the matter!" exclaimed my aunt, shrinking from me and following with her frightened eyes the direction of my gaze. My breath was coming in short, quick gasps now, and my excitement was almost uncontrollable. My aunt cried out:

"Oh, do not look so! You appall me! Oh, what can the matter be? What is it you see? Why do you stare so? Why do you work your fingers like that?"

"Peace, woman!" I said, in a hoarse whisper. "Look elsewhere; pay no attention to me; it is nothing—nothing. I am often this way. It will pass in a moment. It comes from smoking too much."

My injured lord was up, wild-eyed with terror, and trying to hobble toward the door. I could hardly breathe, I was so wrought up. My aunt wrung her hands, and said:

"Oh, I knew how it would be—I knew it would come to this at last! Oh, I implore you to crush out that fatal smoking habit while it may yet be time! You must not, you shall not be deaf to my pleas any longer!"

My Conscience ceased struggling and showed sudden signs of weariness—this pointless meddling with my hardened vice was having a smothering, tranquilizing effect!

"Oh, promise me you will throw off this hateful slavery of tobacco!"

My Conscience began to reel drowsily, and grope with his hands. What an enchanting spectacle!

"I beg you, I beseech you, I implore you! Your reason is deserting you! There is madness in your eye! It flames with frenzy! Oh, hear me, hear me, and be saved! See, I plead with you on my very knees!"

As Aunt Mary sank to her knees, my Conscience reeled again and then drooped feebly to the floor, blinking toward me with heavy eyes a plea of his own—for mercy!

"Oh, promise, or you are lost! Promise, and be redeemed! Promise! Promise and live!"

This last round of my Aunt Mary's meddling did it! With a long-drawn sigh, my conquered Conscience closed his eyes and fell fast asleep!

With an exultant shout I sprang past my aunt, and in an instant I had my lifelong foe by the throat. After so many years of waiting and longing, he was mine at last.

I tore him to shreds and fragments. I shredded the fragments to bits. I cast the bleeding rubbish into the fire, and drew into my nostrils the grateful incense of my burnt offering. At last, and forever, my Conscience was dead!

I was a free man! I turned upon my poor aunt, who was almost petrified with terror, and shouted:

"Out of here with your paupers, your charities, your reforms, your annoying morals! You behold before you a man whose life-conflict is done, whose soul is at peace; a man whose heart is dead to sorrow, dead to suffering, dead to remorse; a man WITHOUT A CONSCIENCE! In my joy I spare you, though I could throttle you and never feel a pang of guilt! Off with you! Fly! Be gone!"

She fled. Since that day my life is all bliss. Bliss, pure bliss. Nothing in all the world could persuade me to have a conscience again. I settled all my old outstanding scores, and began the world anew. I killed thirty-eight persons during the first two weeks—all of them on account of ancient grudges. I burned a house that interrupted my view of the horizon. I swindled a widow and some orphans out of their last cow, which is a very good one, though not, I believe, a thoroughbred. I have also committed scores of crimes, of various kinds, and have enjoyed my work exceedingly, whereas before it would have broken my heart and turned my hair gray, no doubt.

In conclusion, I wish to state, by way of advertisement, that medical colleges desiring assorted cadavers for scientific purposes, either by the gross or per ton, will do well to examine the lot of former missionaries, charity workers, petitioners, carolers, beggars, and peddlers in my cellar before purchasing cadavers elsewhere, as these were all selected and prepared by myself and can be had at a low rate, because I wish to clear out my stock and get ready for the spring trade.

the end

THE FACTS CONCERNING THE RECENT CARNIVAL OF CRIME IN CONNECTICUT

From of the beginning of his long writing and speaking career, Mark Twain was unafraid to speak his mind. He consistently conveyed his exact thoughts on social matters large and small. He was also unafraid to publish often daring and irreverent fiction.

The Facts Concerning the Recent Carnival of Crime in Connecticut is a good example of the latter. It was published in the Atlantic Monthly magazine in June 1876, just months preceding publication of the mischievous, but essentially tame *The Adventures of Tom Sawyer*. Anything but tame, *Carnival of Crime* clearly shows Mark Twain was unafraid to bare his wild side to the world, fully and seemingly without pangs of conscience.

Or at least seemingly without conscience, because this story might be at least partly autobiographical. Twain was deeply affected by the accidental death of his brother Henry and the premature death of his young son Langdon. Even though he had nothing to do with either of their deaths, he tended to believe there must have been something he could have done to prolong their lives.

There is plenty of evidence to suggest that Twain was a big-hearted, compassionate man with deep-seated emotions and great scruples. As such, he was the perfect candidate to be plagued by an over-active conscience.

Running for Governor

A few months ago I was nominated for Governor of the great state of New York, to run against Mr. John T. Smith and Mr. Blank J. Blank on an independent ticket. I somehow felt that I had one prominent advantage over these gentlemen, and that was—good character!

It was easy to see by the newspapers that if ever they had known what it was to bear a good name, that time had gone by. It was plain that in these latter years they had become familiar with all manner of shameful crimes.

But at the very moment that I was exalting my advantage and secretly enjoying it, there was a muddy undercurrent of discomfort "riling" the deeps of my happiness, and that was—the having to hear my name bandied about in familiar connection with those of such people.

I grew more and more disturbed. Finally I wrote my grandmother about it. Her answer came quick and sharp.

She said: "You have never done one single thing in all your life to be ashamed of—not one. Look at the newspapers—look at them and comprehend what sort of characters Messrs. Smith and Blank are, and then see if you are willing to lower yourself to their level and enter a political contest with them. It was my very thought! I did not sleep a single moment that night. But, after all, I could not recede. I was fully committed, and must go on with the fight.

As I was looking listlessly over the papers at breakfast I came across this paragraph, and I may truly say I never was so confounded before.

PERJURY—Perhaps, now that Mr. Mark Twain is before the people as a candidate for Governor, he will bring himself to explain how he came to be convicted of perjury by thirty-four witnesses in Wakawak, Cochin China, in 1863, the intent of which perjury being to rob a poor native widow and her helpless family of a meager homestead and plantain-patch, their only stay and means of support in their bereavement and desolation. Mr. Twain owes it to himself, as well as to the great people whose votes he asks, to clear this matter up. Will he do it?

I thought I should burst with amazement! Such a cruel, heartless charge! I never had seen Cochin China! I never had heard of Wakawak! I didn't know a plantain-patch from a kangaroo! I did not know what to do. I was crazed and helpless. I let the day slip away without doing anything at all.

The next morning the same paper had this–nothing more:

SIGNIFICANT—Mr. Twain, it will be observed, is suggestively silent about the Cochin China perjury. During the rest of the campaign this paper never referred to me in any other way than as "the infamous perjurer Twain."

Next came the Gazette, with this:

WANTED TO KNOW—Will the new candidate for Governor deign to explain to certain of his fellow-citizens (who are suffering to vote for him!) the little circumstance of his cabin-mates in Montana losing small valuables from time to time, until at last, these things having been invariably found on Mr. Twain's person or in his trunk, they felt compelled to give him a friendly warning for his own good, and so tarred and feathered him, and rode him on a rail; and then advised him to leave a permanent vacuum in the place he usually occupied in the camp. Will he do this?

Could anything be more deliberately malicious than that? For I never was in Montana in my life. Yet after this, this journal customarily spoke of me as, "Twain, the Montana Thief.

I got to picking up papers apprehensively—much as one would lift a desired blanket which he had some idea might have a rattlesnake under it. One day this met my eye:

NEVADAS FIRST NEWSPAPER
TERRITORIAL ENTERPRISE
DAN DE QUILLE
MARK TWAIN
Virginia City News
MARK TWAIN
UP TO HIS CADDISH
PRANKS AGAIN!!!

THE LIE NAILED—Three stalwart citizens, Paul Mobafort of Ukranium, and Roger Rocked and Daniel J. Blump of Lickyweakia, have filed sworn affidavits establishing Mr. Mark Twain's vile statement announcing our noble standard-bearer Blank J. Blank's late grandfather had been hanged for highway robbery is a brutal and empty LIE without a shadow of foundation in fact. It is disheartening to virtuous men to see a candidate resort to such shameful means as attacking the dead in their graves and defiling their honored names with slander to achieve political success. When we think of the anguish this miserable falsehood must cause the innocent relatives and friends of the deceased, we are almost driven to incite an outraged and insulted public to enact unlawful vengeance upon the slander monger. But no! Let us leave him to the agony of a wounded conscience (though if passion should get the better of the public, and in its blind fury they should do the slanderer bodily injury, it is but too obvious that no jury could convict and no court punish them for performing that service).

The ingenious closing sentence had the effect of moving me out of bed with haste that night, and out at the back door also, while the "outraged and insulted public" surged in the front way, breaking furniture and windows in their righteous indignation as they came, and taking off such property as they could carry when they went.

And yet I can lay my hand upon the Book and say that I never slandered Mr. Blank's grandfather. More: I had never even heard of him or mentioned him up to that day and date. I will state, in passing, that the journal above quoted from always referred to me afterward as "Twain, the Body-Snatcher."

The next newspaper article that attracted my attention was the following:

A SWEET CANDIDATE—Mr. Mark Twain, who was all set to make such a blighting speech at the mass-meeting of the Independents last night, didn't show up! A telegram from his physician stated that he had been knocked down by a runaway team, and his leg broken in two places—poor suffering man lying in great agony, and so forth, and so forth, and a lot more bosh of the same sort. And the Independents tried hard to swallow the wretched deception, and pretend that they did not know what was the real reason of the absence of the abandoned creature whom they designated their standard-bearer. A certain man was seen to reel into Mr. Twain's hotel last night in a state of beastly intoxication. It is the imperative duty of the Independents to prove that this besotted brute was not Mark Twain himself. We have them at last! This is a case that admits of no shirking. The voice of the people demands in thunder tones, "WHO WAS THAT MAN?"

NEW YORK
CITY

It was incredible, absolutely incredible, for a moment, that it was really my name that was coupled with this disgraceful suspicion. Three long years had passed over my head since I had tasted ale, beer, wine or liquor of any kind. It shows what effect the times were having on me when I say that I saw myself, confidently dubbed "Mr. Shaky Drunkard Twain" in the next issue of that journal without a pang—notwithstanding I knew that with monotonous fidelity the paper would go on calling me so to the very end.

By this time anonymous letters were getting to be an important part of my mail matter. This form was common:

HOW ABOUT THAT OLD WOMAN YOU KIKED OF YOUR PREMISES WHICH WAS BEGING.

POL. PRY.

And this:

MR. TWAIN
There is things
which you Have done
which is unbeKnowens
to anybody but me.
You better trot out a
few dots, to yours tru-
ly, or you'll hear
through the papers from
HANDY ANDY

These are representative examples. I could keep them coming till the reader was filled to the gills, if desirable.

Shortly the principal Republican journal "convicted" me of wholesale bribery, and the leading Democratic paper "nailed"an aggravated case of blackmailing to me. In this way I acquired two additional names: "Twain the Filthy Cheat" and "Twain the Shady Fixer."

By this time there had grown to be such a clamor for an "answer" to all the dreadful charges that were laid to me that the editors and leaders of my party said it would be political ruin for me to remain silent any longer. As if to make their appeal the more imperative, the following appeared in one of the papers the very next day:

B EHOLD THE MAN!—The independent candidate still maintains silence. Because he dare not speak. Every accusation against him has been amply proved, and they have been indorsed and reindorsed by his own eloquent silence, till at this day he stands forever convicted. Look upon your candidate, Independents! Look upon the Infamous Perjurer! the Montana Thief! the Body-Snatcher! Contemplate your incarnate Shaky Drunkard! your Filthy Cheat! your Shady Fixer! Gaze upon him—ponder him well—and then say if you can give your honest votes to a creature who has earned this dismal array of titles by his hideous crimes, and dares not open his mouth in denial of any one of them!

There was no possible way of getting out of it, and so, in deep humiliation, I set about preparing to "answer" a mass of baseless charges and mean and wicked falsehoods. But I never finished the task, for the very next morning a paper came out with a new horror, a fresh malignity, and seriously charged me with burning a lunatic asylum with all its inmates, because it obstructed the view from my house. This threw me into a sort of panic. Newspapers were choking the life out of me!!!

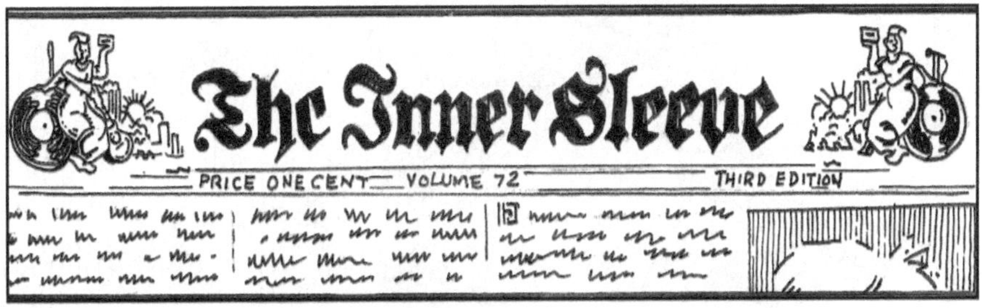

Then came the charge I poisoned my uncle to get his property, with an imperative demand that his grave should be opened. This drove me to the verge of distraction. On top of this I was accused of employing toothless and incompetent old relatives to prepare the food for the foundling' hospital when I warden there. I was wavering—wavering. And at last, as a due and fitting climax to the shameless persecution that partisan rancor had inflicted upon me, nine little toddling children, of all shades of color and degrees of raggedness, were taught to rush onto the platform at a public meeting, and clasp me around the legs and call me PA!

I gave it up. I hauled down my colors and surrendered. I was not equal to the requirements of a Gubernatorial campaign in the state of New York, and so I sent in my withdrawal from the candidacy, and in bitterness of spirit signed it, "Truly yours, once a decent man, but now
"MARK TWAIN, B.S., S.D., F.C., S.F., I.P., and M.T."

the end

RUNNING FOR GOVERNOR

For most of the nineteenth century, politicians funded major newspa-pers throughout the US. In 1870, only 11% of urban daily newspapers were independent of corrupt influence by politicians. Twain surely had this in mind while writing Running for Governor for his monthly column in The Galaxy, a literary magazine, in which he portrayed his fictional candidacy for Governor to be just as hopelessly futile as it would have been in fact. He knew it inevitable that newspaper propaganda generated by both major party candidates in the actual New York election of 1870 would doom any honest candidate to defeat. Ironically, the New York Times ran a series of articles in 1872 that exposed the self-enriching misdeeds of the winning candidate in that election, putting a deserving end to his corrupt political career.

Also, around the time of Twain's column, newspapers had just started becoming largely independent of political funding. But now, more than 150 years later, the foundation on which Twain built Running for Governor—inaccurate news reporting—is again a persistent topic of discussion. Although disinformation has been around forever, the term 'fake news' was not in general usage until 2014. That's when a BuzzFeed News editor began using it to label propaganda that social media sites promoted as real news. These widely circulated, ongoing lies are akin to those which Twain hilariously describes and exaggerates in Running for Governor.

Then came an abrupt twist. A 2016 presidential candidate co-opted and popularized the term 'fake news' when he repeatedly used it to disparage mainstream news reports, usually entirely accurate, that contradicted his statements and examined his actions and proposals. Since that candidate succeeded in getting elected, he voiced the term 'fake news' countless times throughout his presidency and long after he was defeated trying for reelection.

It's pretty easy to guess what Mark Twain might say about the twisted meaning of 'fake news' if he were still around to comment, and it's very easy to wish that he was. Corrupt political leaders in his day inspired him to write satire incisive enough to cut to the core of their deceits and witty enough to provoke audible laughter from his readers. To varying degrees and under many guises, corruption remains an unfortunate feature of democracy. Besides the 'fake news' phenonoma, many present-day politicians and political support systems would inspire Twain's satire. Does anyone doubt he would point his cutting wit their way?

MARK TWAIN
(1835-1910)

Mark Twain was born in Florida, Missouri on November 30,1835 and raised in Hannibal, Missouri, a small town on the Mississippi River. But that's not exactly true. For Mark Twain's legal name was Samuel Clemens, and he was always just plain Sam to family and friends. Mark Twain didn't exist until 1863 when Sam adopted this pen-name while working as a newspaper reporter in Nevada. Soon Mark Twain, author, was writing humorous stories and thought-pieces for readers across the nation. Meanwhile, Mark Twain, lecturer, was cracking-up audiences with finely-polished stories, delivered to perfection. Blessed with remarkable talent for both written and oral story-telling, talents he cultivated with diligent practice, Mark Twain became a famous author and lecturer almost all at once. It didn't take long before Mark Twain's fame spread internationally nor before it became permanent as gold with the publication of *Adventures of Huckleberry Finn* in 1884.

Mark Twain spoke and wrote in a quaint, authentic American dialect with pride and self-assurance at a time when almost all authors thought they needed to stick with high-tone English to earn respect and acclaim. Yet there was something even more crucial to Mark Twain's fame than his innovative literary style; he perfected a method to make people laugh. A serious man at heart, Mark Twain took serious subjects and situations and exaggerated them to a point where potential drama turned into hilarious comedy. His perfection of this comic method caused tears of laughter to wet the cheeks of countless listeners and readers in his day, as it has for generations of readers ever since. Mark Twain became and remains an international treasure mostly because he was so darn funny.

After a long and abundant career, Mark Twain succumbed to heart disease and died in Redding, Connecticut on April 21, 1910. Many millions of fans world-wide mourned his death.

Marc Johnson-Pencook is an illustrator, animator, and muralist. He lives in Minneapolis, Minnesota. His illustrations appear in books, periodicals, gallery shows and private collections, and his murals adorn many walls and ceilings in public places and private spaces in the Twin Cities and beyond. He also teaches illustration at the Atelier Studio Program of Fine Art in Minneapolis and the Art Academy in St. Paul. In addition, Marc composes and performs rock music—he currently plays percussion for "Ozmo Stone"—a rock band based in Minneapolis. Marc can be contacted at: http://illustratormarc.blogspot.com/

Jerome Tiller lives in Minneapolis, Minnesota. He is co-owner of ArtWrite Productions, a publishing company bent on making education and reading more pleasurable for youth. Adapted Classics, an imprint of ArtWrite Productions, uses fine-art illustrations to introduce classic stories to young readers. Learn more about Jerome, his co-owner son Paul, and their company at: artwriteproductions.com and adaptedclassics.com

www.ingramcontent.com/pod-product-compliance
Lightning Source LLC
Chambersburg PA
CBHW030808190726
48285CB00003B/1072
* 9 7 8 1 9 3 9 8 4 6 2 5 9 *